Power of Choice

Written by Christina Karalekas, MST

Illustrator Jonathan Bartlett

AuthorHouse™
1663 Liberty Drive
Bloomington, IN 47403
www.authorhouse.com
Phone: 1 (800) 839-8640

Published by AuthorHouse 02/02/2017

ISBN: 978-1-5246-5844-1 (sc)
ISBN: 978-1-5246-5845-8 (e)

Library of Congress Control Number: 2017900191

Print information available on the last page.

This book is printed on acid-free paper.

authorHOUSE®

Dedication

To my parents, I love you.

&

To all those who feel, or have felt, "stuck."
We can always get "unstuck."
It's a choice. ♥

There are things that
happen to us every day...

But guess what?

I figured out how to solve those problems...
Yup! Yup! I did! Want me to tell you?

Okay, but shh! It's a secret, you can't tell anybody okay?

When I have a problem, I
use my superpower!!

My Power of Choice!

Kind of like mind control! When I don't like something, I choose to change it. I'll show you!

When I feel sad...

I CHOOSE to think of something colorful and happy.

When I feel alone...

I CHOOSE to get up and make a new friend.

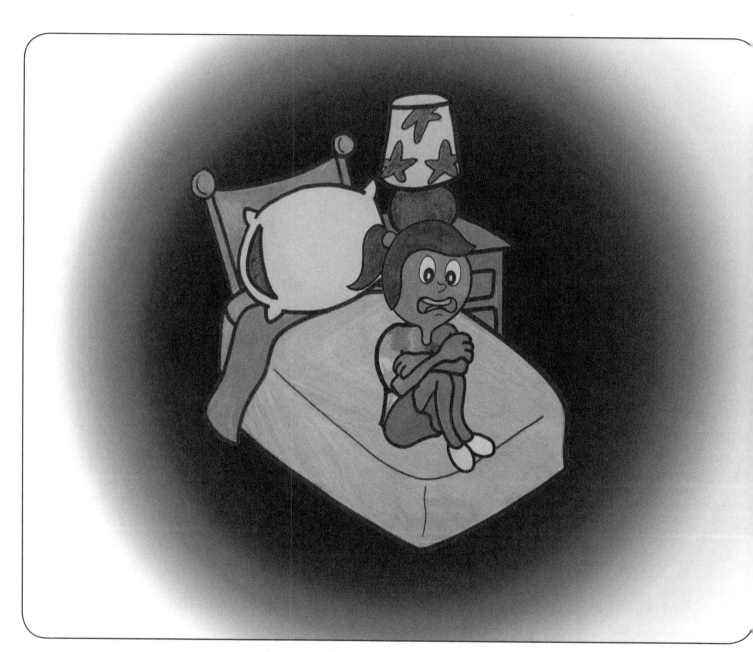

When I'm in the dark...

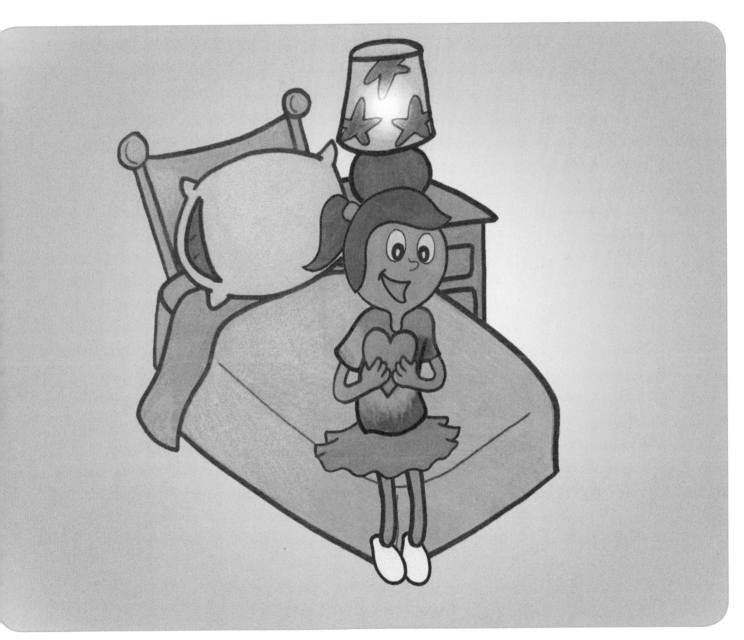

I CHOOSE to find my light.

When I make a mistake...

I CHOOSE to try again.

When I feel overwhelmed or anxious...

I CHOOSE to take
a deep breath, and
ask for a hug.

When I feel scared...

I CHOOSE to put on my invisible cape!

When I want something to look different...

I CHOOSE to use something different.

When I do not like how someone makes me feel...

I CHOOSE to tell them.

When I feel Joy...

I CHOOSE
to share it!

27

But guess what? Here's another secret...
We ALL have this special super power!

Even when you
think you've lost
it, it's there...

You just have to believe...
IN YOURSELF!

CPSIA information can be obtained
at www.ICGtesting.com
Printed in the USA
BVOW05s0708150217
476216BV00004B/6/P